The Original Renewal

No. ....598........

STE-E-E-EAMBOAT A-COMIN'!

WRITTEN BY **JILL ESBAUM**, POET

PICTURES BY **ADAM REX**, CRAFTSMAN

Entered at the Library of Congress, at Washington, D.C., by
Farrar, Straus and Giroux
of New York City

For Mom, Dad, and Greg
In fond memory of our summer vacations BTP
(Before Theme Parks)
—J.E.

For Marie, and for everyone else who posed.
—A.R.

The illustrations and design on the title page are modeled on an 1852
steamboat pilot's certificate from the District of St. Louis.

Text copyright © 2005 by Jill Esbaum
Illustrations copyright © 2005 by Adam Rex
All rights reserved
Distributed in Canada by Douglas & McIntyre Ltd.
Color separations by Prime Digital Media
Printed and bound in the United States of America by Berryville Graphics
Designed by Barbara Grzeslo
First edition, 2005
10 9 8 7 6 5 4 3 2 1

Library of Congress Cataloging-in-Publication Data
Esbaum, Jill.
    Ste-e-e-eamboat a-comin! / Jill Esbaum ; pictures by Adam Rex.— 1st ed.
      p. cm.
    Summary: A village comes to life when a Mississippi River steamboat
arrives and unloads its goods.
      ISBN-13: 978-0-374-37236-1
      ISBN-10: 0-374-37236-5
    [1. Steamboats—Fiction. 2. Mississippi River—History—19th century—
Fiction. 3. Stories in rhyme.] I. Rex, Adam, ill. II. Title.

PZ8.3.E818 St 2005
[E]—dc21
                                                    2002192541

Wavelets lapping,
river wide,
mighty, ever-rolling tide.

Sleepy village,
empty street,
boneless dog with dusty feet.

Napping store clerk,
pesky fly,
distant smudge against the sky.

Floating palace,
white and red,
chimneys belching overhead.

Fiery furnace,
gleaming rails,
paddles churning foamy trails.

Rubberneckers,
pounding boots,
whiskered geezers, big galoots.

Wheels a-clatter,
choking cloud,
yapping dog, excited crowd.

Rumpled jacket,
steady hands,
watchful captain barks commands.

Bells and whistles,
songs and shouts,
burly, brawny roustabouts.

Skim the shallows,
shoreline bump,
fling a line around a stump.

Flying elbows,
reckless crush,
scrambling feet, impatient rush.

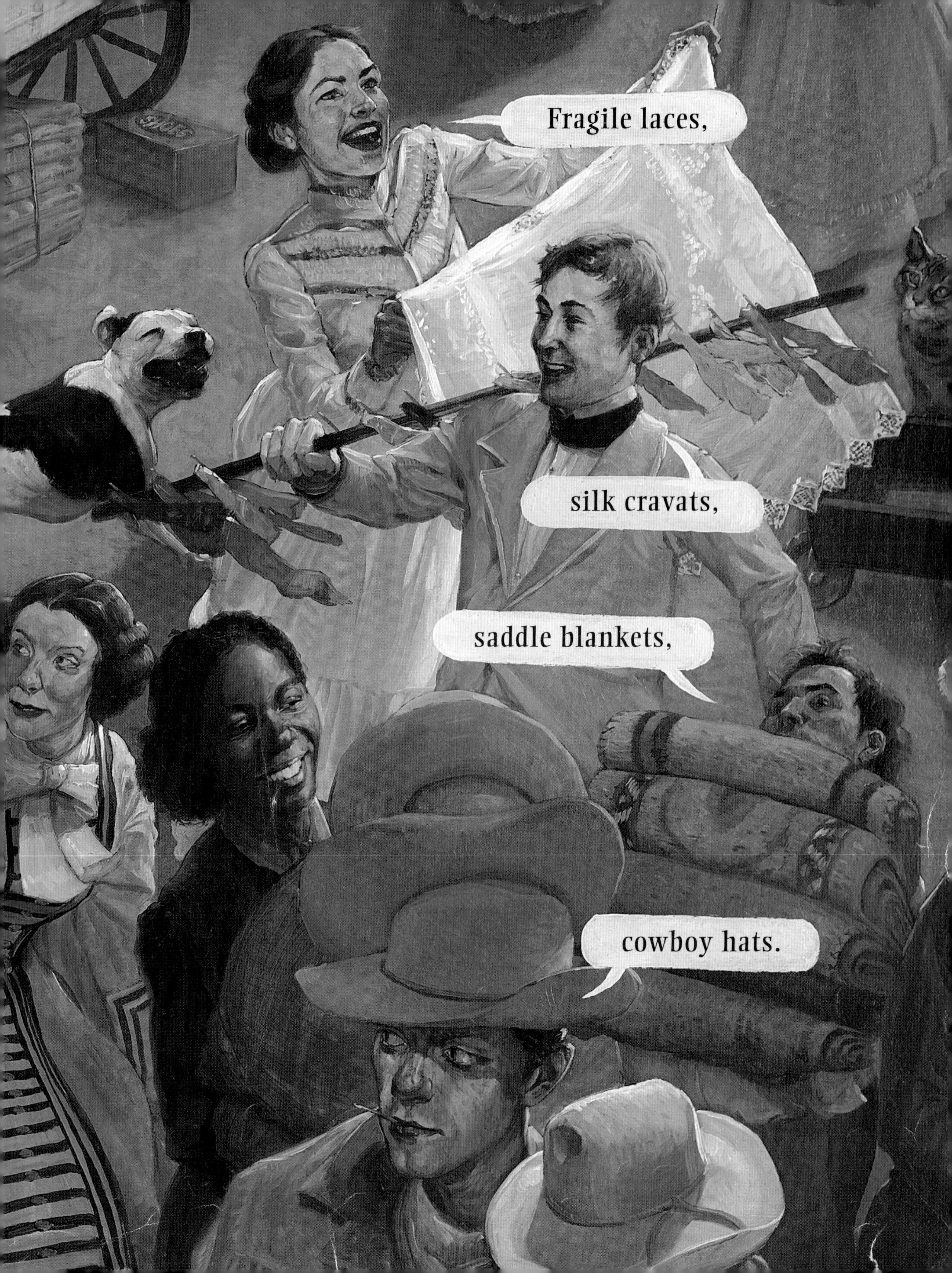
Fragile laces,
silk cravats,
saddle blankets,
cowboy hats.

Warning whistle,
last goodbyes,
hugs and kisses, teary eyes.

Stoke the furnace,
ring the bell,
coil the lines and wave farewell.

Plodding horses,
creaking dray,
slapping paddles back away.

Whippersnappers,
splashing friend,
race the steamboat round the bend.

Shuffling townsfolk,
muggy breeze,
wading heron, bumblebees.

Sleepy village,
empty street,
panting dog with muddy feet.

Wavelets lapping,
river wide,
mighty, ever-rolling tide.

AUTHOR'S NOTE

Sometimes I feel like a time traveler—as on the day I curled up in my favorite chair reading Mark Twain's *Life on the Mississippi*. I turned a page, and suddenly I was standing on a stone-paved wharf in a sleepy 1800s river town. My heart pounded with excitement as I elbowed my way through sweaty neighbors to get a better view of the "floating palace" gliding to shore.

Here's part of Mr. Twain's description of a steamboat visit:

> . . . the white town drowsing in the sunshine of a summer's morning; the streets empty, or pretty nearly so; one or two clerks sitting in front of the Water Street stores . . . chairs tilted back against the wall, chins on breasts, hats slouched over their faces . . .

Then someone would spot a "film of dark smoke" in the distance, and the cry would go up: "S-t-e-a-m-boat a-comin'!"

> . . . the clerks wake up, a furious clatter of drays follows, every house and store pours out a human contribution, and all in a twinkling the dead town is alive and moving. Drays, carts, men, boys, all go hurrying from many quarters to a common center, the wharf. Assembled there, the people fasten their eyes upon the coming boat as upon a wonder they are seeing for the first time.

And once the boat was secured:

> . . . such a scramble as there is to get aboard, and to get ashore, and to take in freight and to discharge freight, all at one and the same time; and such a yelling . . . as the mates facilitate it all with! Ten minutes later the steamer is under way . . . After ten more minutes the town is dead again . . .

I've always lived within a few miles of the Mississippi River and have long been fascinated by its role in the settling of the United States. In writing *Ste-e-e-eamboat a-Comin'!*, I hoped to capture the commotion surrounding a steamboat visit and to show a river town's dependence upon this once-vital lifeline.

The original paddlewheelers may be gone, but you don't have to travel through time to see the Mississippi River. It's still here, as impressive as it always has been: a mighty, ever-rolling tide.